Boomer
Gets His
Bounce
Back

Adapted by Andrea Posner-Sanchez
from the script "Busted Boomer" by Kent Redeker

Based on the television series created by Chris Nee

Illustrated by Mike Wall

 A GOLDEN BOOK · NEW YORK

Copyright © 2013 Disney Enterprises, Inc. All rights reserved. Published in the United States by Golden Books, an imprint of Random House Children's Books, a division of Random House, Inc., 1745 Broadway, New York, NY 10019, and in Canada by Random House of Canada Limited, Toronto, in conjunction with Disney Enterprises, Inc. Golden Books, A Golden Book, A Little Golden Book, the G colophon, and the distinctive gold spine are registered trademarks of Random House, Inc.

randomhouse.com/kids
ISBN 978-0-7364-3143-9
Printed in the United States of America
10 9 8 7 6 5 4 3 2 1

Doc and her friend Emmie are playing soccer. Doc
pretends to be a sports announcer. "World-famous
soccer star Emmie lines up for the kick. She shoots. . . .
She scores!"

Emmie jumps up and down, celebrating her goal.
She gives the ball to Doc. "Hmm, the ball felt a little
squishy when I kicked it," she tells Doc.

"Really? Let me try," says Doc.

Doc kicks the ball. It flies through the
air, but it lands with a weak little bounce and
s-l-o-w-l-y rolls into the net.
  "Way to go, Doc!" shouts Emmie. "You scored a goal!"

But Doc doesn't celebrate. She checks the ball. It is squishier than it should be. "You're right, Emmie," Doc tells her friend. "Something *is* wrong with the ball."

"But we can't stop playing now," says Emmie. "The next kick is for the world championship!"

Doc pretends to be an announcer again.

"Emmie, the best player in the universe, steps up to the ball. Nothing can stop her!"

Emmie gives the ball a BIG kick. But it barely moves. It wobbles and rolls and then stops. It doesn't even reach the net!

Emmie picks up the ball and holds it to her ear. She hears a hissing sound.

"I think it has a leak," Emmie says. "You're the best toy fixer there is, Doc. Can you fix it?"

"I'm pretty sure I can," Doc tells Emmie. "And when I get back, we can finish our championship soccer match."

hissss

Doc goes to her clinic and sets the ball down on the check-up table. She puts on her magic stethoscope. It glows—and all the toys in the room come to life!

"Hi, guys! I'm Boomer," the ball announces.
"I know you! You're the best bouncing ball I've
ever seen!" says Stuffy.

"I love to bounce," Boomer tells all the toys, "but I'm not feeling so bouncy today."

Boomer leaps off the table and lands on the ground with a THUD.

"I should bounce back into the air with a BOING," Boomer says with a sigh. "Why can't I bounce, Doc?"

"I'd like to give you a check-up to see what's going on,"
Doc tells the ball.

Boomer is nervous. "Ooh. A check-up? Uh . . . now that I think
about it, I don't need to bounce."

"You're not scared, are you?" Lambie asks gently.

"No way! I don't get scared. I'm totally not scared," Boomer insists.

"So you'll let me give you a check-up?" Doc asks.

"I guess so." Boomer sighs.

Doc begins the check-up by listening to Boomer's heart
with her stethoscope. "Your heart sounds okay," she reports.

Next, she looks at Boomer's throat with her otoscope.
"Your throat looks fine, too."

When Doc asks Hallie for her next tool, Boomer pulls away and cries, "No, you don't need that!"

"Don't worry. I just need the cuff to check your pressure," Doc tells Boomer as Hallie hands it to her.

"Oh, that. Yeah, go for it," says Boomer, relaxing a bit.

"Hmm . . . Boomer, your pressure is way, way, way down." Doc thinks for a moment and then announces, "Hallie, I have a diagnosis!"

Hallie grabs the *Big Book of Boo-Boos* from the shelf and brings it to Doc.

"Boomer, you have a severe case of Deflate-ulosis!" Doc tells her patient.

Boomer gulps.

"What is that?" asks Lambie.

"Everyone has things that belong on their insides," Doc explains. "Stuffy, Lambie, and Chilly have stuffing. But, Boomer, you're a bouncy ball. You need to be full of air to bounce right."

Doc reaches into her doctor bag. "The first thing I need to do to cure Deflate-ulosis is patch your leak."

Boomer holds still as Doc covers the hole with a patch. "Thanks, Doc! Now I'm ready to go back and play!" Boomer says.

"Not yet," says Doc. "I still have to put more air back inside you."

"Naw, that's all right. I'm good," Boomer claims as he tries to roll away.

Doc thinks she knows why Boomer is scared. "Have you been filled with air before?" she asks the ball.

Boomer nods.

"And you know I'm going to use an air pump?" Doc asks as she pulls a pump from her doctor bag.

"And it has a needle," Boomer says with a sigh. "I'm scared of needles!"

Doc explains that she has to use the needle—it's the only way to fill Boomer back up. Chilly jumps in front of Doc. "Oh, no! I think I need more air inside me, too!" he claims.

"Chilly, you're not a ball," Doc reminds him. Then she turns back to Boomer. But he's gone!

Doc and the toys look all over for Boomer. Finally, Lambie finds the ball hiding inside the dollhouse. "I think you need a cuddle," she tells him as she gives him a big hug.

Doc kneels next to Boomer. "Want to know a secret? When I need to get a shot with a needle from *my* doctor, I'm always scared," she admits. "But my mom comes and gives me a big hug, and that helps me to be brave."

"I like hugs," says Boomer.

"We could *all* give you a hug!" suggests Lambie.

"That should help you feel brave," Doc says.

Hallie, Lambie, Chilly, and Stuffy give Boomer a big hug. Boomer says he feels better already. "Let's do this!"

Doc inserts the needle and starts pumping. "You're being really, really brave!" she tells Boomer.

Boomer starts to get **bigger** as he is filled with more air. "I can feel myself getting bouncier and bouncier!" he shouts.

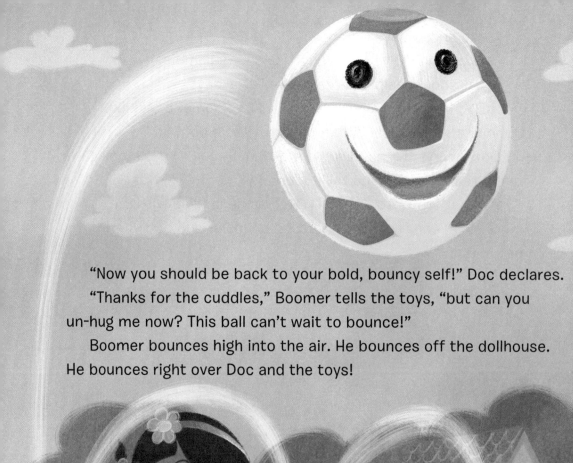

"Now you should be back to your bold, bouncy self!" Doc declares.

"Thanks for the cuddles," Boomer tells the toys, "but can you un-hug me now? This ball can't wait to bounce!"

Boomer bounces high into the air. He bounces off the dollhouse. He bounces right over Doc and the toys!

"Thank you, Doc!" Boomer yells as he continues bouncing. "I don't know if you knew this, but I *love* bouncing!"

"Aren't you glad you were brave?" asks Stuffy.

"I sure am," admits Boomer. "A few seconds of being brave and now I'm back to bouncing way, way, way high! This is great!"

Doc giggles. "It's great to have you back in bouncing shape," she tells the happy ball. "Now let's go meet up with Emmie so we can finish our world championship soccer match!"